Perfectly Natalie

An Inspirational Children's Christmas Story

Sandra L. Cole

Illustrated By:
Rodney Johnson

Balboa Press books may be ordered through booksellers or by contacting:

Balboa Press
A Division of Hay House
1663 Liberty Drive
Bloomington, IN 47403
www.balboapress.com
1 (877) 407-4847

ISBN: 978-1-4525-1620-2 (sc)
ISBN: 978-1-4525-1621-9 (e)

Printed in the United States of America.

Balboa Press rev. date: 06/20/2014

It is with deep love that I dedicate this book to
my children and grandchildren.

You are my greatest gifts.

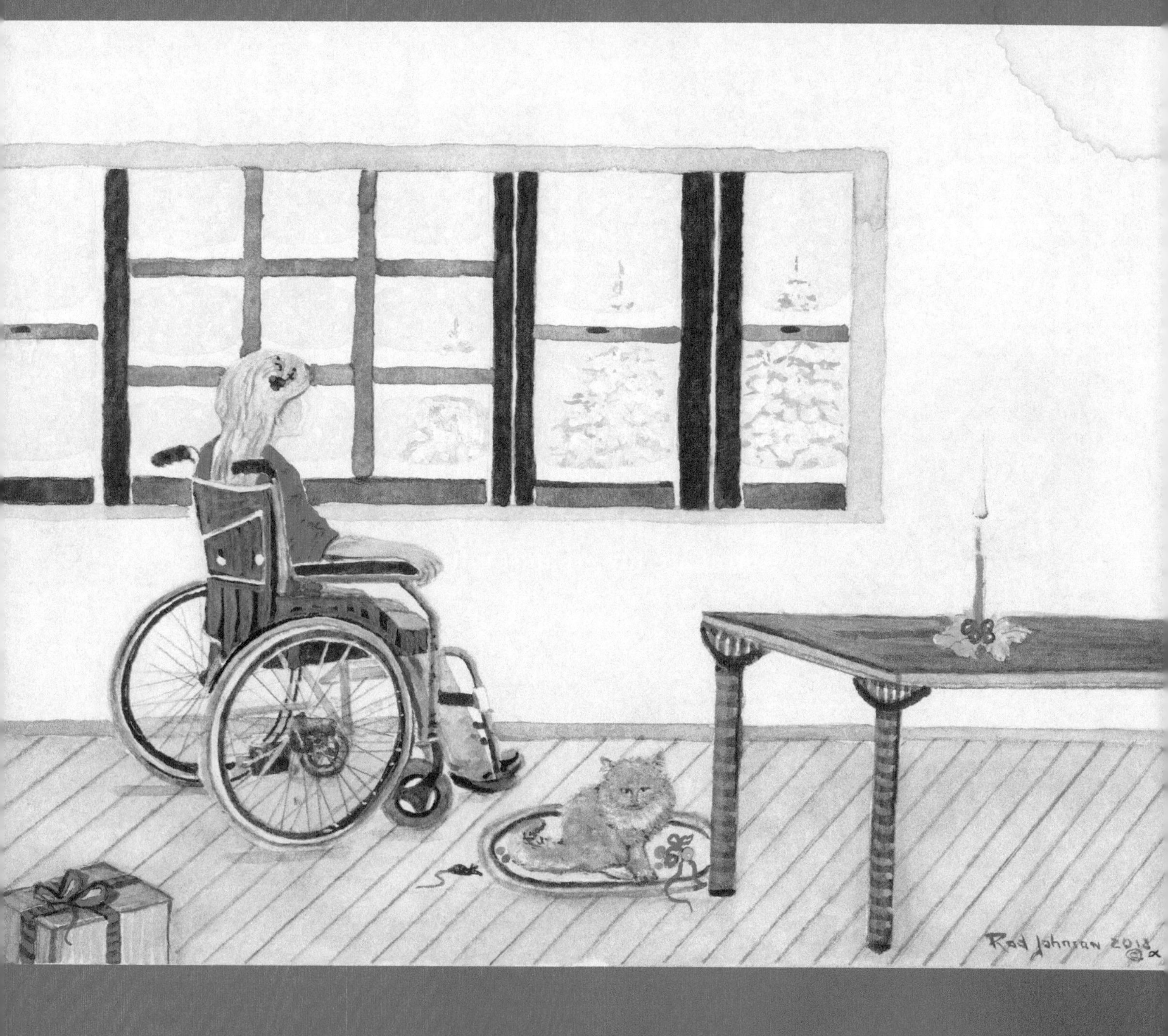
Rod Johnson

My name is Natty. My real name is Natalie, Natalie Christianson, but you can call me Natty. I don't like Natalie. I used to like it, but it's so—so perfect sounding. Daddy named me Natalie. He always calls me Natalie, his "perfect little angel." Well, I'm not perfect! I used to be, but now my legs don't work right, so you can call me Natty. Oh, they work a little (I have leg braces and crutches), but they're heavy and slow, so I spend most of my time in this dumb ol' wheelchair.

I used to run and play with Scotty McPherson next door and Rebecca Abrams down the block, but that was last year, when I was in first grade. That was before the accident. I guess I was riding my bike too far out in the street. I don't remember too well. I remember waking up in a room with people all around me. It was a hospital. They cheered when I opened my eyes. I had to stay there a whole month—yuck! The doctors and nurses were real nice to me, and I even got ice cream, but I couldn't wait to go home. Ever since then, though, my legs haven't worked quite right. Somethin' about nerve damage, whatever that is. So now I'm stuck here in this crummy ol' chair while my friends, or my used-to-be friends, are out playing in the snow. And if that isn't bad enough, it's only two days till Christmas. This is going to be a crummy Christmas!

Rebecca came by yesterday to tell me what she's hoping to get for Christmas. Can you believe it? Yep! Designer jeans with a Lee label on the back pocket. She's sure she's getting a new Ken to go with Barbie, too. Well, whoop-de-do! Who cares about designer jeans anyway? I suppose her jacket will have a label too.

Scotty just left. He's all excited about the bike he saw in Penney's Toyland department. It's red and white, with no training wheels, and it has a horn with three tones. Can you believe it? Three tones! Whew! Ahhhhh, who cares! My bike didn't have training wheels either, and who wants a three-toned horn anyway?

"Natalie, I'm home."

It's Dad. There he goes, calling me Natalie.

"Get your jacket. We're going to get a tree. Natalie, where are you? Oh, there's my perfect little angel. Why aren't you out helping Mom pack our lunch?" he asked me.

"It's Natty, Dad!"

"What, Natalie?"

“It’s Natty! Call me Natty!”

“Oh, okay. Natalie, let’s get your mittens on, and here’s your scarf. We’ve got to bundle up warm because it’s cold outside.”

“Dad, what are you doing? I can’t go pick out a Christmas tree!”

“Of course you can. Mom has lunch packed, including your favorite cookies. I have the saw, and we’re ready to go.”

“No, Dad, I don’t want to go!”

“But why? We go every year.”

“You know! This dumb ol’ chair. It won’t be the same,” I said sadly.

“Ohhh, that’s it. Well, Natalie—”

“It’s Natty!”

“Okay, Natty, let me tell you a little secret. You’re right, it won’t be the same; however, we have gone every year since before your first Christmas to pick out our tree. I carried you into the forest when you were a baby, and I’ll carry you again today. We’re a family, and this is a family outing. And now, little angel, you need to get a positive attitude and make this a fun trip.”

“What’s a positive attitude?”

Dad thought for a moment. “It’s telling yourself, ‘I’m going to make the best that I can out of this trip! Whether I can walk or not, I’m going to have fun.’ And then you do it! Look for the fun and good things. Not the fact that your legs aren’t well yet.”

“Yet? They’ll never be well!”

“Natalie, positive attitude.”

“It’s Natty,” I said with a frown.

The trip only took thirty minutes since the Christiansons lived at the base of a mountain that was covered with trees. Mr. Christianson was a forester, and he knew the woods well. Natty remembered how much fun she used to have when they'd go pick out a tree. She and Dad would climb all over the hill looking for that perfect tree. The limbs had to be even, without even one missing, and the top had to be just right so Mom's angel would stand perfectly at the top. Natty loved the snow and loved to help Dad cut the tree down. When they were finished, Mom had hot soup and sandwiches to warm them up and Natty's favorite cookies for dessert—butter cookies shaped like Santa, frosted in red and white. It was so fun. At least it used to be.

I don't know about this "positive attitude" stuff, Natty thought, *but I don't see how we can have any fun now.*

Mr. Christianson pulled the truck off the highway, down a logging road and into a snow-covered clearing. Natty knew this area well. For as long as she remembered, they had come here each Christmas to look for a tree and in the spring and summer for picnics—except for last spring and summer, because of the accident. In the summer, the meadow was alive with butterflies and birds singing. The grass was green and full of wildflowers, and there was a stream where the deer came to get a drink. In the winter, the meadow was a blanket of white, and the air was silent.

"Come on, Natalie—Natty," Dad said as he cradled her in his arms and started off into the woods. "Keep your eye out for that perfect tree."

They hadn't hiked far when Mr. Christianson found a large stump that made a nice perch for Natty to sit and see all the trees. Getting her settled and secure, Mr. Christianson stepped back a few feet and said, "Okay, Natalie—Natty, which one looks good?"

Natty couldn't help but smile. Dad always made things fun, and he looked so silly with those long legs sinking deep in the snow. He went from tree to tree asking Natty how they looked. Were the branches all straight, and was the top level? Natty studied the trees from her perch but found herself particularly drawn from all the symmetrical ones to a small tree that was being crowded out by bigger ones.

TREE FARM
Rod Johnson
2013

"How about that one, Dad?" Natty hollered across the snow.

Mr. Christianson hobbled through the deep snow toward the direction Natty was pointing.

"Which one, Natalie? These are all too big."

"Look, Dad, the smaller one … there, that's it, Dad, that one."

"This one?" Dad asked, questioning his daughter's choice.

"Yes, Dad, I like it."

"Ohhh," said Dad, stepping back and looking over the tree, "but Natalie, look, it's missing some limbs, there's a bend in the trunk, and the top isn't level for Mom's angel. It's not perfect, and there are others so much better."

The word "perfect" stuck in Natty's heart. She knew about being "not perfect."

"It's Natty, Dad, and I like it."

Mr. Christianson sat down next to Natty and studied the misshapen tree his daughter had chosen. Perplexed by Natty's choice, Mr. Christianson questioned her decision.

"Can you tell me why you like it better than that one?" Dad said, pointing to a lovely, perfectly shaped tree nearby.

"It looks lonesome," said Natty with a sad face. "I bet nobody would ever pick it."

No wonder, Dad thought.

"It will be beautiful, Dad, when it's all decorated."

Mr. Christianson studied his daughter's face and wondered why this tree was so important to her. Noticing his questioning look, Natty said, "Dad, maybe you need to get one of those things. What did you call it? Pos … posi … positive something."

"You mean a positive attitude?" Dad said with a chuckle.

"Yes, that's it! You need a positive attitude."

"You're right, little angel," Dad laughed. "I really need one!" he exclaimed, and he cut down the tree.

When Mom saw Dad heading back with Natty in one arm and dragging the tree with the other, she hurried up the hill to help them. They giggled and laughed about previous treks up the hill, remembering great family times they'd shared. When they arrived back at the truck, Dad set Natty in her chair while Mom got out lunch. The hot soup and sandwiches really hit the spot, especially since they were topped off with Natty's favorite cookies.

After lunch, Mom said, "Hold up the tree so I can see it."

Dad waited silently for his wife's reaction. Natty held her breath. Mom slowly looked the tree all over, up and down and all around. After what seemed like forever, Dad asked, "What do you think?"

Mom looked at Dad, then looked at Natty, and then she said with a smile, "Oh, I think it will be lovely."

Natty wasn't sure her mom meant it, because moms always talk like that, but Natty was sure the tree was meant for them.

As they drove back to town, Mom asked Dad to stop at the shopping mall so she could pick up some last-minute things.

"I'll stay in the car," Natty said as Mr. Christianson pulled into a parking place.

Mr. Christianson knew that Natty hadn't been out in public in the wheelchair. "Oh, come on, Natty," Dad said. "Let's check out the toy department."

"No!" said Natty. "I don't want to go!"

Surprised by his daughter's defiance, Mr. Christianson knew Natty needed to get out and face people. So despite Natty's protests, Dad placed her in her chair and wheeled her into the mall.

The mall was full of life. Christmas carols rang merrily through the stores. Each shop window was decorated with festive lights and animated characters. Despite Natty's scowl, shoppers were smiling and laughing as they greeted others in the holiday spirit. Natty couldn't help but notice all the designer jeans on the rack as Dad guided her chair through the girls' department on the way to the toys. Turning the corner, Natty saw the red-and-white bike that Scotty had told her about. She grabbed for the horn as Dad pushed her by. He stopped to let her squeeze it. Beep! Beep! Beep! Three tones, just like Scotty said. Just past the bike display were shelves stacked high with Barbie and Ken dolls with all their accessories. Natty looked very carefully at all the new outfits. Her eyes stopped on a new Ken. His hair was styled differently, and he was dressed in a ski jacket and pants. Natty was sure that this was the Ken Rebecca wanted. Across the aisle were trucks and cars of all makes and sizes. Hot Wheels and lowriders, fastbacks and diesels. *Boy stuff,* thought Natty. *Bet this is Scotty McPherson's favorite place.*

When Mr. Christianson turned down the next aisle, Natty gasped. Right in front of her, in all his glory, sat Santa Claus. Natty reached down and yanked the wheel of her chair so the chair swiftly turned to the left.

"What are you doing?" Dad said with surprise.

"I don't want him to see me!"

"Who?"

"Santa Claus. I don't want him to see me like this."

"Natty," Dad said, kneeling down beside her, "Santa doesn't care if you are in a wheelchair."

"How do you know?" Natty said sharply.

"Because Santa isn't like that. He loves all children. He doesn't care if you can run or jump. He loves children that can't see or hear, even children who have no arms or legs."

Natty's eyes filled with tears as she rolled her chair down the aisle to the Cabbage Patch Kids.

"Natty," Dad said as he caught up with her, "each one of us is special. God gave all of us a special gift to share with the world. Even people who can't talk or walk still have something special to share, and when you shut yourself off from the people around you, you cheat us out of your special gift. Mom and I love you; so do your friends and even Santa Claus. We love you—just because you are you."

Natty stared at the Cabbies and thought about what Dad had said. She wanted to believe him, but what if he was wrong? One thing was for sure: she didn't feel special.

"I have to run over to the auto department. Do you want to stay here till I get back?"

Natty nodded.

DOLL

When Dad was out of sight, Natty turned her chair slowly around and inched her way back down the aisle. She came to a spot where, if she sat real straight in her chair and peeked through the Christmas Wonder Dolls, she could see Santa Claus and the children gathered around him. She heard him giggle and laugh with each child, and he always added a "Ho, ho, ho!" Natty couldn't help but notice that the next child in line had a cast on his leg. When it was his turn to sit on Santa's lap, Santa got up from his chair and reached his big arms out to lift the boy up into his lap. Santa even placed the cast over his other knee so the boy was comfortable. Then Santa joked and laughed with him, just like he did with the other children. *Maybe Dad is right,* thought Natty. *Maybe Santa doesn't care if we're perfect.*

"Hi, little angel," Dad said. "What ya looking at? Can you see Santa?"

"Oh, no," said Natty, "I was just looking at the Wonder Dolls. Can we go home now?"

"Yes," Dad said. "Mom's all through shopping. Would you like to stop and see Santa before we leave?"

"No, let's go." *I hope he remembers me as I was last year,* Natty thought as Dad wheeled her from the mall.

It had been a full day. When dinner was over, everyone was ready for a good night's sleep. When Natty awoke, it was Christmas Eve morning. Natty would have known it was Christmas Eve even if she hadn't been aware of the date because of all the wonderful smells filling her room. It smelled of pumpkin, cinnamon, and evergreen. It made Natty excited because she knew what the day held in store. Natty pulled her chair close to her bed so she could lower herself into it. Then she headed for the kitchen.

"Well, good morning, sleepyhead," Mom said as Natty wheeled into the room. "Did you have a good night's sleep?"

"Yes," Natty said as her mom handed her a glass of milk.

"Dad's out decorating the tree if you want to give him a hand."

Natty smiled as she propped the glass between her legs and headed for the family room. Christmas Eve was always a special day. Mom baked all kinds of special treats that she only made at Christmas, and Dad and Natty decorated the tree.

"Natalie—Natty," Dad said as she entered the room, "come help me with these ornaments. I need your help with the tree."

Natty wheeled over by the tree and gave it a long, hard look. Dad had the lights on as best he could, but there were some bare spots that were giving him trouble. Natty felt a kinship with this tree. She knew it was special, so she backed away a few feet and started instructing Dad as to where the ornaments should hang. They hung ornament after ornament, which filled the tree with a special wonder. Even Dad seemed to get caught up in its magic. When the last ornament was placed, it was time for Mom's angel. When Dad placed it on the top, it drooped and sagged and tilted, not at all like an angel should.

"Take her off, Dad. Angels are perfect; she can't sag. We'll have to think of something."

"Well, Natty, you knew the top of this tree was uneven when we cut it. There's a limb missing. I suggest we drill a hole and glue a small branch here to replace the missing one," Dad said, pointing at the gap.

"But that isn't right," Natty said. "The tree didn't grow that way. It doesn't seem right to change it from what it is. Can't we pin her skirt to the branches or something?"

Dad studied the top of the tree and the angel as he grumbled under his breath. "A pin won't work. I think the limb idea is best."

Natty frowned.

"Well, I'll see what I can find." With that, Dad was off to the garage. After a few minutes, he was back with some wire, still grumbling.

"What are you going to do?" asked Natty.

"Just give me a minute," Dad said.

Natty could tell he was concentrating. Mr. Christianson worked with the angel and the top of the tree for several minutes. Except for an occasional "Oops," Dad didn't talk. Natty waited quietly.

Then Dad stepped down from the stool and said, "Ta-daaa!"

Natty's eyes grew wide with delight, and her smile radiated with magic. It was the smile that was only Natalie's. Dad hadn't seen that smile since before the accident.

"How'd you do it, Dad?" Natty said, bursting with joy. "She's beautiful!"

"Oh, you know," Dad said, stammering, "it just took a … some, a …"

"Some of that 'positive attitude' stuff?" Natty said with a wink.

Dad laughed loudly. "Yes, little angel, a positive attitude."

"She is beautiful. Look at her—doesn't she look like she's floating above the tree? It's almost like she's watching over all of us."

"She is, Natty, I know she is."

Dad gave Natty a big hug as they looked over their tree.

"Well, little angel, this is not the tree I would have chosen, but you were right. It seems to have a special energy, and it is beautiful."

Natty beamed with pride.

"Guess I'll read the paper," Dad said as he started to relax in his chair.

"But Dad."

"Hmmm?"

"What about the Dickens Village? Aren't we going to put it under the tree?"

"Uh huh," Dad mumbled as he sank deeper into his chair. "Soon."

Natty knew Dad would be engrossed in the paper for a while. That was typical of dads when they needed a break. So Natty wheeled herself to the coffee table, where the Dickens Village lay wrapped carefully in boxes. She began opening each box and imagining where each house should be placed. The village was special to Mom. Natty remembered that each year, Mom bought a new piece for the village. She didn't seem to care if there were presents under the tree for her; a new house in the village seemed to be all she wanted. Mom loved the village, and it created a special world under the tree. Each Christmas, the shops and people came out of their boxes and brought a piece of England into the Christiansons' home.

Natty sorted through the boxes carefully and unpacked the church, the schoolhouse, the bakery, and the barbershop. Natty particularly liked the people who made the village come to life. She unwrapped the policeman, the clergyman, the baker, and the teacher and set them on the table for Dad to place under the tree.

"Come on, Dad, we need to place the village for Mom."

"I'm almost done," Dad mumbled from behind the paper.

Natty couldn't wait any longer, so she loaded her lap with the shops and people and headed to the tree. Stretching and reaching from her chair, she placed the village under the tree. It wasn't quite right, but it was the beginning of a Dickens Village. *Something is missing,* Natty thought, *but what is it?* She turned her chair around and noticed a small box on the edge of the table. She wheeled herself over to it, opened it, and looked inside. Sure enough, it was Mom's favorite piece. It was a mother, father, and child, dressed warmly and wearing ice skates, just like Natty and Mom and Dad used to do. Natty was excited to get it placed under the tree, so she grasped the figurine in her hand and wheeled herself merrily toward the tree. Unfortunately, the figurine slipped from her fingers and hit the floor. Dad looked up from his paper, and Mom came out from the kitchen. There sat Natty, looking down at the broken village family.

Rod Johnson
2014 ©

“I’m sorry,” Natty said as she began to cry. “I didn’t mean to.”

“I know,” Mom said as she picked up the pieces.

Natty could tell by the tone of her voice that Mom was sad. Natty wished that she could somehow make it right. “I should have been more careful,” Natty said as her mom headed toward the kitchen.

“Accidents happen,” Mom replied.

“Wait, Mom, please don’t throw them away.”

“They’re broken, Natty. I’ll look for a new set next year.”

“No,” Natty said, choking back her tears. “Please let me have them.”

Mrs. Christianson saw how sincere Natty was, so she brought the pieces back and placed them in her hand. Tears rolled down Natty’s cheeks as she looked at the once beautiful family. The mom’s head was broken off, one of the dad’s arms was broken, and the child’s hat was chipped. As Natty looked at the pieces, she realized they were not the perfect mother, father, and child they had been for years in the Dickens Village.

“Here,” Mom said, reaching for the pieces, “let me throw them away.”

“No,” Natty said, holding them tightly, “they were special.”

Dad peeked over his paper and gave Mom a wink, like dads do when they’re letting moms know it’s okay.

“All right,” Mom said, “but don’t get cut.”

“Thanks,” Natty said, wheeling herself and the Dickens family off to her room. Later, Natty returned with the figurine. The mom’s head was back, the dad’s arm was set, and the chip off the child’s hat was replaced. Natty handed them to Dad and asked him to place them under the tree.

Noticing the glued pieces didn’t fit quite right, he said, “Are you sure you don’t want us to buy a new one?”

"No," said Natty. "Not everyone is perfect in our town, and probably not everyone was perfect in the real Dickens Village either, but they are still a family."

Dad smiled at his daughter's wisdom and placed the family under the tree.

Christmas Eve was busy. People were in and out; Mom ran around town delivering Christmas treats, and grandmas and grandpas called from far away. The day passed quickly, and as evening approached, Scotty and Rebecca came by with Christmas gifts. Natty gasped as they handed her presents because she hadn't even thought about gifts for them. Without a moment's hesitation, Mrs. Christianson reached under the tree and handed gifts to Scotty and Rebecca.

"Oh, thank you, Natty!" they each said.

"Thank you," Natty said as she looked at her mom.

"You open yours first," Rebecca said to Natty.

Natty tore into her gift to find a new Ken inside the paper. "Oh *wow*!" Natty said. "Thanks. You open yours."

Rebecca opened her package to find a beautiful snowsuit with boots and goggles for her snow bunny Barbie. "Oh, thanks, Natty. I needed these!"

"Okay, Scotty, you open yours."

His package was already half open, and inside was a fancy black Corvette with flames on the sides. It made a grinding noise as he pushed it along the floor. "Wow!" he said as he pushed it around the dining room. "You open yours!"

Natty opened the box to find a license plate that said "NATALIE" on it. Natty looked at it curiously.

"I picked it out myself," Scotty said with pride. "It's for your bike. When you can ride again, you'll have your own license plate."

"Thanks, Scotty," Natty said with a lump in her throat. "When I can ride again."

"Well, guys," Mom said, "it's time to go home. It's getting late, and tomorrow is a big day. Merry Christmas."

"Merry Christmas," Scotty and Rebecca hollered back.

Natty placed the license plate on her nightstand and the new Ken beside her in bed. "Thanks, Mom," Natty said as her mom tucked her into bed.

"For what?"

"For buying presents for Rebecca and Scotty. I guess I hadn't thought much about gifts this year."

"You're welcome. I understand."

"I love you, Mom."

"I love you too, Natty. Sweet dreams."

Natty looked for a long time at the license plate that Scotty had given her. How she had loved to ride with him. Finally, she drifted off to sleep and dreamt of riding a new bike with her own license plate on it.

It's amazing how wide-awake you can be early on Christmas morning. The clock on Natty's dresser read 6:10 a.m. Natty thought that was early, but it *was* Christmas. She listened for any noise from her parents. It was pretty quiet, except it sounded like someone was in the kitchen. Oh, and maybe those were Dad's footsteps in the hall.

"Hello," Natty said, trying not to yell too loudly.

"Hello," came an answer from the hall. "Merry Christmas, little angel," Dad said as he peeked into Natty's room.

"Merry Christmas!" Natty said, struggling to put on her robe.

"Are you ready to see what Santa brought you?"

Natty gulped at the thought that Santa remembered her. What would he bring? She hadn't written a letter or even talked to him in the mall. How could he know what she wanted or where she lived? She wasn't even sure what she wanted.

"That's it," Dad said as he sat her in the chair and straightened out her robe. As he wheeled her down the hall, Natty laughed because Dad was singing a Christmas song, and he never knows the right words. As they passed the kitchen, Mom joined them with cups of hot chocolate with marshmallows on top. Mom joined Dad in the song, but *she* knew the words.

DAD
Natalie
MOM
Rod Johnson

Gradually, they turned into the family room—and Natty saw it. It was a bike! Not just any bike—it was the red-and-white bike, just like Scotty McPherson wanted. Natty grabbed the wheels of her chair and raced over to the bike. She ran her hands over the fenders and handlebars and then the horn. It even had a horn! She beeped it. Then she beeped it again and again. Wow! A three-toned horn. She could hardly believe it. Then Natty pulled away from the bike and looked at it in anger. The tag hanging from the handlebars said, "Love, Santa."

"Why did Santa bring me a bike?" she cried. "I can't ride a bike. If he loved me, he'd know I can't ride a bike!"

"No, Natty," Dad said firmly, "Santa sent you a bike because he knows you *can* ride a bike."

"I can't ride a bike; my legs don't work right!"

"That's right, Natty, but they will work correctly if you'll just try."

"I have tried!"

"Yes, Natalie, you have tried—a little, but you need to set your mind to it. Remember that 'positive attitude' stuff? You can do it!"

There it was again. That name, "Natalie," and those words, "positive attitude." Natty wheeled herself closer to the tree. Mom and Dad sat silently, sipping their hot chocolate and letting Natty think. Finally, Dad began handing out the presents. The pile in front of Natty grew and grew. It was hard for Natty, even in a wheelchair, not to be excited. The grandmas had sent lots of things—grandmas are like that—and there were gifts from relatives Natty hardly knew.

Mom and Dad started opening presents; there was music playing, and they were laughing. Natty fidgeted in her chair and suddenly couldn't stand it any longer. She started tearing through presents one after another. There were more gifts than she could imagine. When Natty finally reached the end of the presents, she looked at the lot that lay before her. There were dresses for Barbie, outfits for Ken, T-shirts and sweatshirts that were just her size. The last package she opened was a pair of jeans. Yes, designer jeans with a Lee label!

“Eeeyeow!” Natty squealed. “Mom, could you help me get dressed?”

“You bet,” Mom said, following Natty to her room. She helped Natty out of her chair and onto the bed and then watched as Natty struggled to remove her robe and pajamas.

“Need help?” Mom asked as she watched Natty struggle to push and shove her legs into her new jeans.

“No, I can do it,” Natty said, almost out of breath from the job she was performing. When she was through, with only a little help from Mom, Natty was dressed in a new pink T-shirt and designer jeans. “Can you brush my hair, Mom?”

“Sure,” Mom said as she brushed the long, blonde locks of her lovely little girl. “All ready?” Mom said, preparing to place Natty in her chair.

“No, Mom,” Natty said, “not the chair. Let’s try the braces.”

With great surprise, Mom helped Natty strap the braces on her legs. Then, with an “I-can-do-it” look, Natty took her crutches and struggled to her feet. She picked up the license plate off the nightstand and placed it in her pocket. Then Natty looked back at Mom and said, “I’m ready.”

Tears of pride filled Mrs. Christianson’s eyes as she opened the door.

“Wait, Mom, does my label show?”

Mom looked quickly for a price tag that might have been overlooked.

“No, Mom, my label, on the back of my jeans. Can you see the label?”

“Oh yes,” Mom said with a laugh, “it shows up *real* clear.”

With that, Natty dragged her legs down the hall to the family room. When Dad saw his little angel struggling to take steps, his eyes filled with tears of happiness and pride. When Natty got within a few feet of him, she handed him the license plate.

DAD
MOM
DOLL

Mr. Christianson scooped her up in his arms and held her tight. “Oh, Natty, you are going to ride that bike.”

“Yes, Dad, I am!”

“This is a very special Christmas, Natty,” said Dad. “You know, I learned something from you.”

“You did?” Natty said, thinking that Dad already knew everything.

“I learned that a tree doesn’t have to be perfect to be beautiful and full of magic.”

“I learned something too, Dad.”

“What’s that?”

“I learned that you don’t have to be perfect to be loved and that sometimes we all need some of that ‘positive attitude’ stuff.”

“Boy! Is that right, little angel,” he replied, and they both laughed and looked at their tree.

“I love you, Natty.”

“I love you too, Dad. Oh, and Dad … you can call me Natalie.”